W9-CHL-132

For Willy,
a dog like Claude

CLARION BOOKS
Ticknor & Fields, a Houghton Mifflin Company

Copyright © 1974 by Dick Gackenbach
All rights reserved. Printed in the United States of America.

Library of Congress Cataloging in Publication Data

Gackenbach, Dick.
Claude the dog; a Christmas story.

SUMMARY: Claude, the dog, gives away all his
Christmas presents to his down-and-out friend but
receives an even better present from his young owner.
[1. Dogs—Fiction.   2. Christmas stories]   I. Title.
PZ7.G117C1   [E]   74-3403
ISBN 0-395-28792-8   Paperback ISBN 0-89919-124-X

Previously published by The Seabury Press under ISBN 0-8164-3116-7

Y 10 9

CLAUDE THE DOG

A CHRISTMAS STORY

WORDS & PICTURES BY DICK GACKENBACH

CLARION BOOKS
TICKNOR & FIELDS : A HOUGHTON MIFFLIN COMPANY
NEW YORK

"Merry Christmas, Claude."

"We didn't forget you. See!"

"Here's a dog pillow from Momma."

"A dog blanket from Poppa."

"And a rubber mouse from me."

"That's all. Be a good dog, Claude."

Along came Bummer. He had no home.

"Look at all my presents, Bummer."

"My! You are a lucky dog, Claude."

"See my soft pillow, Bummer?"

"Never saw a pillow, Claude.
I sleep on the hard ground."

"Here, you take my pillow, Bummer."

"Oh, thank you, Claude."

"See my nice warm blanket, Bummer?"

"Never saw a blanket, Claude.
My nights are very cold."

"Then you take my blanket, Bummer."

"Thank you, Claude!"

"See my toy? It's a rubber mouse, Bummer."

"Never had a toy, Claude.
Sometimes I get very lonely."

"Then take my rubber mouse
to keep you company, Bummer."

"But you have no presents left, Claude."

"My best present is at home, Bummer."

"You've made me so happy, Claude.
I wish you a very Merry Christmas."

"Merry Christmas to you, Bummer."

Thump!

Crunch!

Slurp!

"We love you, Claude."